Geronimo Stilton

THE INVISIBLE PLANET

Scholastic Inc.

D0028880

Published by Scholastic Inc., *Publishers since 1920*, 557 Broadway, New York, NY 10012. SCHOLASTIC and associated logos are trademarks and/or registered trademarks of Scholastic Inc.

ISBN 978-1-338-21504-5

Text by Geronimo Stilton
Original title *Il pianeta invisibile*
Cover by Giuseppe Facciotto (pencils) and Flavio Ferron (color)
Illustrations by Giuseppe Facciotto (pencils), Carolina Livio (inks), and Serena Gianoli and Paolo Vicenzi (color)
Graphics by Marta Lorini

Special thanks to Shannon Decker
Translated by Julia Heim
Interior design by Kevin Callahan / BNGO Books

10 9 8 7 6 5 4 3 2 1   18 19 20 21 22

Printed in the U.S.A.   40

First printing 2018

THE SHATTERMOUSIX

It was a calm cosmic afternoon: no solar storms on the horizon, no planets in danger, no urgent appointments in my digital calendar. In fact, the universe was so calm that Grandfather William had even given me a few hours off to rest!

Holey space cheese, I could finally write some more of my epic novel: The Amazing Adventures of the Spacemice. Oh, excuse me — I haven't introduced myself! My name is Stiltonix, Geronimo Stiltonix, and I am captain of the *MouseStar 1*, the most mouserific spaceship in the universe. (It's a fabumouse job, even though my secret dream is to be a WRITER. Shhh — don't squeak!)

As I was saying, I had been trying to finish my **novel** for eons, but it's not easy to write when you're the captain of a spaceship. Some sort of cosmic chaos is always popping up!

THE Amazing Adventures of the Spacemice

I was feeling fabumousely focused on my writing when someone **KNOCKED** on the door of my cabin.

Galactic Gorgonzola, who could it be?

I turned and saw my cousin Trap, my nephew Benjamin, and his friend Bugsy Wugsy all standing in the doorway.

"Hey, Cousin!" Trap said with a grin. "Why are you sitting here, molding like old

Plutonian provolone? We need to scamper over to Astral Park right away!"

I scratched my snout, confused. "WHY?"

"You mean you don't know, Uncle?" Benjamin squeaked excitedly. "Today a rattastic new ride is opening!"

Hey, Cousin!

Who's there?

Bugsy Wugsy piped in. "And we're going to try it out!"

"You'll come with us, won't you, Uncle G?" they both cried at once.

I really wanted to keep writing, but I couldn't **disappoint** my favorite mouselets!

I nodded and got to my paws. "Oh, all right . . ."

As we scampered toward **Astral Park**, Trap said, "I'm impressed, Cousin—for once, you're not acting like a cheesebrain! You'll see, a little adventure will do you good."

I didn't understand a cosmic cheese rind of what he was squeaking about. "Umm . . . **ADVENTURE?**"

Trap grinned. "I knew you wouldn't be **scared** of a few steep declines, super sharp-as-cheddar curves, and a dozen or so acrobatic tailspins . . ."

WhaT?!

Super steep declines?! Sharp-as-cheddar curves?! Acrobatic tailspins?! Oh, for all the galaxies in the universe, my whiskers were trembling in fear!

Trap didn't seem to notice. "We're going to have so much fun on the ShatterMousix!"

The ShatterMousix? **Squeeeeak**—the name alone twisted my tail in knots!

A moment later, I stood in front of a supertall, supersteep, superscary roller coaster.

Benjamin smiled. "It's out of this world, right? I can't wait to ride it!"

RIDE IT? I was frightened out of my fur just looking at it!

We'd almost reached the front of the line when HOLOGRAMIX, *MouseStar 1*'s onboard computer, appeared in front of me.

"Code yellow! Code yellow! Code yellow!

Captain, you need to return to the control room at once!"

I couldn't help breathing a sigh of relief. I was saved!

Move It, Geronimo!

Breathless, I raced to the control room, followed by Trap, Benjamin, and Bugsy Wugsy.

As soon as we entered the room, Grandfather huffed, "Took you long enough, Grandson! What were you so busy doing instead of being the **captain** of this ship?"

Where were you, Grandson?

I stammered, "Hello, Grandfather . . . I . . . Actually . . . Remember I had the afternoon off . . . to write my book? And then the ShatterMousix—"

"What are you squeaking

about, afternoon off? What book? What ShatterMousix? You are the captain of this ship, Geronimo! Anytime there's an emergency, you need to get to the control room at once. No, you need to be here already! The whole crew is counting on you. Have I made myself clear?"

"Yes," I squeaked, hanging my snout.

"Good! Now get a move on! We have a mystery to solve!"

A mystery? Oh, for all the planets out of orbit, what was my grandfather squeaking about now?

Just then my sister, Thea, called me over. "Geronimo, there's something strange going on. Come look at the radar."

I approached and studied the screen

carefully, but it looked like the usual **INTERSTELLAR SPACE** view to me!

"**I DON'T SEE ANYTHING STRANGE!**" I admitted.

Grandfather William glared and yelled in a booming voice, "You wouldn't notice a **meteorite** if it smacked you on the snout!" He enlarged the star quadrant on the screen. "Look again."

I concentrated and saw a *planet* suddenly appear on the radar. It was sparkling and strangely shaped. It looked almost like . . . a **lock**!

I pointed to the screen. "What's this? That planet just appeared out of nowhere! Wait a whisker-loving minute—now it's not there anymore! It VANISHED!"

On the radar screen, the planet I'd been pointing my paw at was gone!

I rubbed my eyes in disbelief. A moment later, the lock-shaped planet reappeared.

For all the satellites in the solar system, Grandfather was right — this was a mousetastic mystery!

1 The mysterious planet appeared on the screen.

2 The mysterious planet disappeared from the screen.

Planet Lockix

At that moment, our onboard scientist, Professor GREENFUR, entered the control room. He peered at the screen. "Cosmic cheddar, that's the planet LOCKIX! So it does exist!"

What in the universe was he squeaking about? I turned to Thea for an explanation, but she seemed just as **surprised** as me!

"Planet Lockix?" she repeated. "I've never heard of it!"

"It disappeared from the galaxy's radar years ago," Professor Greenfur explained. "But it has reappeared. That's

Lockix exists!

incredible! I had only read about Lockix in astro-geography books—and now here it is, on our own radar. My whiskers are *wobbling!*"

Grandfather William scratched his snout. "The history of this planet is awfully *mysterious*. I want to know more!"

We consulted the *Encyclopedia Galactica*, but the information about Lockix and its inhabitants was awfully vague.

Strange, very strange!

Benjamin asked, "Why did the planet **disappear**?"

Bugsy Wugsy asked, "Why isn't there a photo of its inhabitants?"

And Trap added, "Why isn't there any information about the aliens' favorite **food**?"

Thea scolded him. "Trap, does this seem like the time to worry about food?"

From the Encyclopedia Galactica
THE EH-HEMS

Planet of Origin: Lockix
Traits: These aliens are extremely reserved. They are very small and are known for their lack of physical strength, their dubious nature, and their resourcefulness.

Yum, yum!

"It's as good a time as any!" my cousin answered, munching on a chunk of Martian mozzarella cheese that he'd found in a drawer of the control room.

I held up a paw. "This situation is complicated. We need to understand what's happening on Lockix, and the *Encyclopedia Galactica* doesn't have much helpful information."

Meanwhile, the mysterious planet kept **appearing** and DISAPPEARING from our radar screen.

Grandfather William looked at the radar, then at Greenfur, and then at me . . .

Cosmic cheesy chews, I recognized that

look on his face—it meant **out-of-this-world trouble** on the horizon!

Just as I suspected, Grandfather announced, "Grandson, we're facing a MYSTERY of enormouse proportions— and you need to organize an expedition to solve it!"

LEAPING LIGHT-YEARS! WHY DO THESE THINGS ALWAYS HAPPEN TO ME?

THE CATCHIX

In the control room, everyone was enthusiastic about taking an expedition to the disappearing planet—everyone except me! I couldn't help it; I was flooded with fear . . .

What if we fell into a **BLACK HOLE**? Or ended up in the middle of a magnetic storm? Or ran into PiRaTE sPaceCaTS on Lockix?

Thea looked up from the radar and interrupted my thoughts. "Geronimo, we have a problem! Lockix is disappearing and reappearing on the radar screen so quickly that I can't get its COORDINATES to map out a route."

For all the lunar cheese, had I understood

her right? It was impossible to map out a route to Lockix? Stellar Swiss balls . . . what fabumouse news!

I was about to breathe a sigh of relief when Greenfur squeaked up. "Don't worry, I have a solution! I'll go get my latest INVENTION."

Rats! For a nanosecond there, I'd thought that I would be able to go back to writing in my cabin!

Greenfur scampered off to his LABORATORY and returned with a strange contraption. "This is the **catchix**, a frequency catcher."

We must have looked cosmically confused, because he continued, "Thanks to a strong radar signal

The catchix!

calculations system, this device computes all the false data and multiplies it by the frequency of the signal. Adding the cosmic constant will give a perfect result!"

Umm . . .

STINKY SPACE CHEESE . . . WHAT?

But Thea seemed to understand perfectly. "You're full of surprises, Professor! Can you explain how we use it?"

Greenfur smiled PROUDLY. "It's enormously easy! Just stick the catchix's suction cup to the radar screen. In a few astroseconds, it will capture the exact POSITION of the planet!"

Professor Greenfur activated the device, which let out a sequence of sounds.

Beep! Beeep! Beeeep!

After a few moments, the professor proudly announced, "There, it's done!"

Lockix's coordinates had **APPEARED** on the monitor!

Grandfather William nodded, satisfied. "Thea, warm up the *EXPLORATION SHUTTLE'S* motors. Get ready to leave in two shakes of a mouse's tail!"

MISSION INVISIBLE PLANET!

"Uncle, you're going to the invisible planet!" Benjamin exclaimed. "That's rattastic! Can I come?"

Bugsy Wugsy joined in. "I want to come, too—we could do a PROJECT about this mysterious planet! Maybe we could even help update the information in the *Encyclopedia Galactica*."

Both mouselets peered up at me hopefully.

Leaping light-years! How could I say no?

I threw my paws in the air. "Oh, all right—you can come! But promise me you'll be careful. Unexplored planets can be danger—"

I didn't finish my sentence because just then Sally de Wrench, our official onboard mechanic, appeared! (She was the most fascinating rodent on MouseStar 1, paws down.)

"Fabumouse timing, Sally!" Trap cheered. "You're just the **EXPERT** rodent to help us on our mission!"

Being around Sally made me turn red from the ends of my ears to the tip of my tail.

Sally smiled at me. "Hello, Captain! Was there something you wanted to tell me?"

I felt my knees wobble like sonic string cheese, but I tried to get a grip. "N-no, my m-mission—I mean, the in-invisible planet—I mean—"

What can I say? I feel like I'm bouncing through an asteroid belt every time I see Sally . . . and I end up making a fool of myself!

Finally, I took a deep breath and said, "The shuttle motors are up and running. It's time for us to leave for the invisible planet!"

We headed for the shuttle as fast as our paws would carry us! Everyone chatted enthusiastically, but I couldn't help moving a bit more slowly than the others.

I don't know why, but I had the terrible feeling that we were headed for a *galaxy of trouble*!

We're off!

Something's Missing . . .

After traveling for a **galactic hour**, we entered the orbit of the invisible planet.

"Here we are – Lockix!" Thea squeaked.

As my sister steered us toward the surface, we admired the landscape through the shuttle windows. There were ultramodern buildings, roads, squares, elevated walkways—and everything was shaped like a key, a lock, a keyhole, or a safe!

Bugsy Wugsy's eyes were wide. "Stellar Swiss balls—I've **never** seen any place like this!"

Mousetastic!

"Uncle, I'm so happy we came!" Benjamin squeaked, tugging on my sleeve. "Look down there—an enormouse **galactic space park** shaped like a key!"

Bugsy Wugsy added, "This planet looks like it has everything a rodent could want."

"*Something's missing*," Thea muttered quietly.

Trap rolled his eyes. "What are you squeaking about, Cousin? This place has everything! I can't wait to land!"

I looked down at the surface of Lockix, then over at Thea. There didn't seem to be anywhere to land. I peered at the planet again and asked, "WHERE'S THE SPACEPORT?"

My sister shook her snout. "Exactly, Geronimo! I've looked everywhere—there isn't one!"

We circled the planet over and over. There didn't seem to be anywhere to land!

Swiss supernovas! How could there not be a single **spaceport** on Lockix? And how in the galaxy would we get down there?

An Acrobatic Landing!

Thea continued flying over Lockix, looking for a safe place to land, but it was more difficult than tracking down rare Martian mozzarella! First, Thea **steered** us to the right to avoid a lit-up building. Then she **PULLED** the shuttle upward and turned left to **avoid** a satellite dish.

Holey craters, I think I would have preferred to ride on the **ShatterMousix**! I grabbed my seat belt with both paws

Hold on!

and tried not to toss my cheese.

Benjamin and Bugsy Wugsy, on the other paw, were having a blast. "**Yahoo! Mouserific!**"

Finally, Thea squeaked, "I found just the place! Hang on—we're going in for a bumpy landing!"

The ship *DESCENDED QUICKLY* toward a large square, and Thea maneuvered us expertly.

I squeezed my eyes shut, and . . .

Bam!

I heard a bang, jumped in my seat, and then . . . silence.

RAT-MUNCHING ROBOTS! WHAT HAD HAPPENED?

We're here!

I opened my eyes slowly, and . . . cosmic cheese chunks, we had landed safe and sound in the center of the big square!

We climbed off the space shuttle and looked around in amazement. It definitely seemed like the first time in many cosmic eras that someone new had landed on Lockix.

But where are the inhabitants?

"This is so exciting!" Benjamin said. "No **SPACEMICE** have ever visited this planet! I can't wait to meet its inhabitants."

I scratched my snout. "Yes, but . . . where are its **inhabitants**?"

Just then we heard a noise behind us. We spun on our paws and . . .

"It looks like someone's coming to

Hee, hee, hee!

Ha, ha, ha!

Ho, ho, ho!

welcome us!" Trap whispered loudly.

Sure enough, a group was approaching us, but these aliens were not what we had imagined . . .

The *Encyclopedia Galactica* had said that the Eh-Hems were tiny and reserved, but the creatures coming toward us were enormouse, noisy deceptiods. There must have been some kind of MISTAKE!

WHO ARE YOU?

One of the aliens stopped a few steps from me. He sneered and showed his teeth. Black holey cheese, he smelled like one of the *cosmic algae* concoctions that Squizzy, our onboard cook, often whipped up!

"Foreigners!" he said. "Who are you, and what brings you to our tiny *planet*?"

At those words, the smell of *galactic garlic* and Martian mushrooms mixed with Trap's dirty socks hit me. Cosmic cheese chunks, it took my breath away!

I took a deep breath and gathered myself. "We are the **SPACEMICE**, and

Foreigners!

I am Geronimo Stiltonix, captain of the *MouseStar 1*. We noticed that your planet was appearing and disappearing from our *radar*, so we have come to help you!"

The alien snickered. "Help us? I am Claw, the captain of the Uh-Huhs—no, wait—what is it we call ourselves?" Another alien WHISPERED something in his ear. "Ah, yes, I meant to say the Eh-Hems! That's us!"

The group of aliens at Claw's back began to giggle and jab one another with their elbows.

Strange, very strange!

We spacemice all looked at one another in confusion, but Claw went on. "We have been living on this planet for astrocenturies . . . for galactic eras . . . Well, since forever!"

The group of aliens held back more LAUGHTER.

Claw concluded, "We are so sorry that you interfered—uh, I mean, worried about us and our planet."

STRANGE. VERY STRANGE!

My friends pulled me aside. Thea was very suspicious. "How is it possible that they don't know the **NAME** of their own species?"

Sally nodded her head in agreement. "The *Encyclopedia Galactica* said that they were **TiMiD AND SHY**."

"They seem to be the OPPOSITE of timid and shy!" Trap scoffed.

Was it possible that, for the first time ever, the *Encyclopedia Galactica* was wrong?

WEAK AND DEFENSELESS!

We were still unsure of what to do with the MYSTERIOUS aliens. Suddenly, Thea squeaked, "I've got it! We can call Hologramix and ask it to double-check the *Encyclopedia Galactica*! There must be an explanation in there somewhere."

"That's a great idea," I said, nodding. "Activate wrist communic—"

But before I could finish, Claw waved his paws in the air.

"Stop! Halt! Freeze!"

Holey craters, what now?

Claw went on with a smile. "You can't call your **SPACESHIP**. Communication with outside planets or vehicles is strictly prohibited on our planet!"

mousey meteorites!

Thea narrowed her eyes. "Why, exactly, is it forbidden?"

"Well, outer space is full of traps, dangers, and space pirates," explained Claw. "They could find us by intercepting just one communication! We are so . . . um . . . weak and defenseless . . ."

Galactic Gorgonzola, had he said defenseless?

These aliens seemed anything but defenseless to me!

Claw's friends began to chuckle again, but he gave them a look. "It's for our own protection that we've kept our planet INVISIBLE all this time."

"How exactly did you do it?" Sally asked.

The alien grinned. "Easy! We used a PLANETARY INVISIBILITY SYSTEM to keep ourselves hidden from galactic radar. It's been flawless . . . until today!"

Sally's eyes sparkled with curiosity. "Holey craters, I would love to see it. What MOUSERIFIC technology!"

The alien sighed. "Yeah, it was a superrefined technology, but now the system is **broken**! That's why the planet appeared on your radar. And without the Planetary Invisibility System, we're doomed to be **invaded** by some evil passersby before long."

Cosmic cheese rays, how **terrible**!

But I couldn't help wondering . . . Why were all the other deceptiods sneering even more now?

STRANGE, VERY STRANGE!

Claw smiled sweetly. "By any chance, would you spacemice be able to help us?"

"Yes, well, um—what would we have to do?" I asked.

Ha, ha, ha!

"We could use your help repairing our Planetary Invisibility System," Claw said.

"You seem to have a lot of resources, while we are just weak and DEFENSELESS aliens. If we don't fix the system soon, who knows what will attack us?"

All the other deceptiods nodded in agreement, still *GIGGLING*.

Oh, for all the lunar cheese, what could I say?

A TRUE CAPTAIN

As I thought, I remembered the words that Grandfather William had repeated during my first days as captain:

1. A true captain never backs away from a space mystery!
2. A true captain always offers to help aliens in trouble!
3. A true captain always knows the right thing to do!

So I took a deep breath and said, "Of course we'll help! Sally, our supersmart mechanic, will surely be able to fix your Planetary Invisibility System."

Sally smiled at me. "Thanks, Captain!"

I turned as red as **spaghetti sauce** from Saturn while Sally looked back at the aliens.

I'll fix it!

"Take me to your Planetary Invisibility System, and I'll figure it out!"

The **DECEPTiODS** peered at one another for a moment. "We . . . umm . . . well . . . We don't know where it is."

Cosmic cheese rays, did I hear that right? The inhabitants of LOCKIX didn't know where their own Planetary Invisibility System was?

"The Planetary Invisibility System is hidden," Claw explained hastily. "It's secret! Unreachable! For reasons of . . . INTERPLANETARY SECURITY."

This explanation smelled funnier than space cheese!

"Only our technician knows where it is,"

Claw continued. "But he's . . . absent at the moment."

Thea twirled her whiskers. "Absent?"

One deceptiod responded, "That's right! He's exploring a satellite biosphere!"

Another yelled, "He's studying the paths of *MASSIVE METEORITES*!"

And another chimed in, "He has a lunar cold!"

Oh, for all the planets out of orbit—they had each said something completely different!

Strange! Enormously strange!

Claw said, "Our technician is absent, and

all we have is the **instruction manual** for the Planetary Invisibility System. There should be a map in the manual that shows how to reach the system, but we can't figure it out."

"Bring me the manual," Sally suggested. "Maybe I can decipher it!"

Claw clapped her on the shoulder. "Thanks! You are truly a bunch of foo—um, **SUPERSWEET HEROS!**"

He sent one of the deceptiods to get the manual, and Thea pulled me aside. "Geronimo, doesn't this seem **strange**? These aliens don't know the name of their own species, they're completely different from the way they were described in the *Encyclopedia Galactica*, and they don't have a cheesecrumb of a clue where their PLANETARY INVISIBILITY SYSTEM is. What in the galaxy is going on here?"

I couldn't shake the feeling that we were missing some very important information. "You're right, Thea, but these aliens really seem to be in trouble. Plus, I gave them my word as captain—I can't take it back now!"

My sister nodded. "All right, but let's stay alert. This seems like a fur-brained scheme to me!"

I had a feeling that GALACTIC TROUBLES were on the horizon . . .

THE PLANETARY
INVISIBILITY SYSTEM

The deceptiods returned after a few minutes, carrying an ELECTRONIC MANUAL that looked like a tablet.

One of them shrugged. "See? There are so many **BUTTONS**! Without our technician, we can't seem to get it open."

Sally had already gotten to work. In no time, she unlocked the manual and began to scroll through its contents. Cheesy comets, what a brilliant mouse!

When she finished reading, she said, "This is just a simple instruction manual. There's a map that shows how to get to the Planetary Invisibility System, see? It even indicates which antitheft devices are activated along the way."

"Antitheft? I hope they aren't d-d-dangerous!" I squeaked, shivering.

Claw took me under his arm. "Don't be scared—we'll go with you! Surely you'll need the guidance of us Scal—I mean, us Eh-Hems!"

He put his other arm around Sally's shoulders and led us down the path mapped out in the **manual**.

Before long, we arrived in front of a small building. When we set paw inside, we found ourselves standing before a mysterious TUNNEL.

One of the deceptiods snickered. "Please, guests first!"

I gathered my courage and stepped forward, just as Sally yelled, "Captain, wait!"

WHOOOOSH!

A gust of wind tickled my fur.

"What's happening?" I squeaked in alarm.

I took a few steps farther, and —

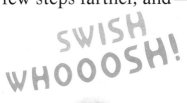

Another gust of wind sent me flying through the air!

SWOOSH
SWISH
WHOOOSH!

Cosmic cream puffs, I was struck by a real windstorm! Now I couldn't go forward at all, not even a whisker-length!

Trap grabbed me by the ear and ordered, "COUSIN, GET DOWN!"

Sally came forward, yelling, "Captain, this

is the first **antitheft device**! It's an air-activated floor. You need to **DODGE** the airbursts to move forward!"

I knew one thing—this wasn't going to be easy!

Thanks to their size, the aliens could move forward easily, and my fellow spacemice **dodged** the airbursts fabumousely. With Trap's help, I finally managed to reach the end of the tunnel. My fur stood on end.

I had made such a terrible impression!

Run, Captain!

We continued on our way and eventually arrived at the entrance to a room with a floor curved like a frying pan.

"This is strange," I muttered.

I didn't have time to say more because Claw pushed me forward with his tail and boomed, "Proceed, mouseoid! You go first!"

I tumbled forward and noticed that the walls were curved, too! The chairs, desks, and other furniture were all nailed to the ground.

STRANGE, VERY STRANGE!

I entered the room and tried to take a few steps, but—squeak! It was cosmically complicated!

Now, I'm not a very sporty mouse, but I

really couldn't manage to move my paws forward at all! How **MYSTERIMOUSE** . . .

Suddenly, I noticed that the ground was no longer beneath my paws—it was slowly moving upward! Black holey cheese! The room began to **roll faster, and faster, and faster**. It felt like I was inside a supersonic washing machine! **HEEEELP!**

Sally squeaked out, "This is the **SECOND antitheft device**! It's a reverse spin-cycle room. Captain, to stop it, you need to press the red button on the wall!"

I was **SCARED** out of my fur, but I knew I had to follow Sally's directions. I began to **RUN** like an athlete in the Great Galactic Games, as fast as my paws could take me. With a lot of effort (and even more **sweat**!), I finally managed to press the button.

As quickly as it started, the room stopped spinning. The other spacemice, along with the aliens, easily walked across to me.

"YOU WERE GREAT, UNCLE!" Benjamin cheered.

Captain, press the red button!

Come on, Uncle!

My muscles felt as wobbly as cream cheese pudding, but I was happy.

Sally pushed on a nearby door and said, "WE MADE IT! Here's the Planetary Invisibility System. Fabumouse job, Captain!"

Pant! Pant!

WHAT AN EXTRAORDINARY RODENT!

The door led into a laboratory. In the middle of the room was an enormouse computer surrounded by a huge tangle of wires.

Sally walked up to the computer and carefully analyzed it.

"I have **mousetastic news**!" she said. "I know this system—I studied it at the Plutotechnic University of Ultraphysics and Galactic Mechanics! It's based on a voice-generator model."

Claw smirked. "It doesn't seem like it has much of a voice to me. This thing is quieter than a **BLACK HOLE**!"

All of the deceptiods **laughed** loudly.

Sally thought for a moment. "Usually, voice systems are really big chatterboxes. If yours is quiet, it's only because . . . it's been jammed!"

"**JAMMED?**" the aliens said. They were suddenly interested.

"Exactly — the system went into overdrive and then turned off," Sally explained. "But it's functioning. You just need a quick **reboot** to make it talk like before!" Sally grabbed her **multifunctional pocket tool** and began working on the computer, jumping from one side of the enormouse machine to the other.

Leaping light-years, what an extraordinary rodent!

My crush on Sally was growing! I have to admit, I was watching her so closely that I hardly noticed Claw WHISPERING something to his friends.

Psst, psst . . .

Ah, what an extraordinary rodent!

Suddenly, a noise snapped me out of my trance—

BIP! BIIIP! BIIIIIP!

The supercomputer let out a sequence of sounds and then lit up like a CLUSTER OF STARS!

Galactic Gorgonzola, Sally had done it!

"HOORAY!" Bugsy Wugsy cheered. "That was marvemouse! I want to become a mechanic just like you, Sally."

I was proud of Sally and smiled shyly at her. She smiled back, which made me melt like cosmic cheddar too close to the sun.

Cheesy comets, what a mouse!

I was twisting my tail into knots when a voice BOOMED over the loudspeakers.

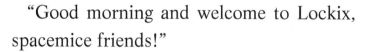
"Good morning and welcome to Lockix, spacemice friends!"

Starry space dust, the Planetary Invisibility System had found its voice — and it was superpolite!

"I would like to thank you for the work you did **fixing me**. It is quite a pleasure to meet you! I would very much like to chat with you, but I must warn you that shortly before your arrival, Planet Lockix was invaded by the Scaleers. They are large, deceptiod aliens . . . and they are extremely DANGEROUS!"

Cosmic cheese chunks, did I hear that right?

Claw and the aliens we had met weren't the real inhabitants of Lockix. Thea was right! Suddenly, all of the strange things that had happened made sense! And now . . . **We were in danger!**

Black holey galaxies,

PLANET LOCKK HAD BEEN INVADED!

A GALAXY OF TROUBLE!

The Scaleers surrounded us, but Thea stood up tall. "I knew you were hiding something!"

Claw stepped proudly forward and began to SNICKER. "Well, yes, we aren't the ha, ha . . . I mean the hee, hee . . . you know, the ho, ho . . . Basically, we aren't the real inhabitants of this silly little planet!" He sharpened his nails. "We are the **Scaleers**, the most ferocious, most clever, and most dangerous space pirates in the whole universe. Thanks to the malfunctioning PLANETARY INVISIBILITY SYSTEM here, it was easy for us to land and take

over Planet Lockix! And now, thanks to you
Spacemice, we can make sure no other mice
find this place again. It's ours!"

We were dealing with some real **cosmic
creeps**!

Sally narrowed her eyes. "Why were you
so interested in Lockix?"

Claw chuckled. "We need a base for our

From the Encyclopedia Galactica
THE SCALEERS

Planet of origin: Slimedox

Profession: Space pirates

**Traits: Aggressive, ferocious, and
love to snicker**

**Motto: "You can tell a good day by
its spoils!"**

RAIDS, and this planet is perfect for that. We can hide our stolen loot on Lockix, and no one will be able to find it! Who would ever think to look on an **invisible planet**?"

The other Scaleers burst into rowdy applause. However, Thea wasn't intimidated. "You're just a gang of **space scoundrels**! You won't get away with this!"

Claw looked at her with a wicked smile on his scaly face. "Oh, you

You won't get away with this!

galactic fools! Just what do you think you're going to do about it? No one will be able to come rescue you, thanks to your help with the Planetary Invisibility System . . ."

Stellar Swiss balls, the Scaleer captain was right!

We had helped a gang of space scoundrels, and now we were their prisoners. We were in a GALAXY OF TROUBLE!

TRAPPED!

Suddenly, something occurred to me. "WH-WHAT H-H-HAPPENED TO THE R-R-REAL INHABITANTS OF L-LOCKIX?" I stammered.

"That is a very interesting question, indeed," Claw said.

"Wh-why?" I squeaked.

"Because it's the same thing that's going to happen to you!" he exclaimed, laughing. He turned to his companions and ordered, "*GRAB THEM!*"

Rat-munching robots, I was frightened out of my fur!

As quick as comets, the Scaleers surrounded us. They led us to a big building cloaked in darkness.

One of them waved an arm at the building.

"Welcome to the Lockix megastadium!"

As we went inside, another added, "Don't try any tricks! There are always guards watching the doors. There's no escape!"

Then the Scaleers left, locking the enormouse door behind them.

I was squeakless. We were trapped!

Wait one whisker-loving minute—we weren't all here! Where were Benjamin and Bugsy Wugsy?

Thea noticed the panicked look on my snout. "I saw them slip away," she said quietly. "I'm sure they're safe!"

PHEW! At least my beloved nephew and his friend weren't trapped in this horrible place with us!

I sighed. "Mousey meteorites, we're done for! We'll never be able to stop those space scoundrels . . ."

At that moment, a 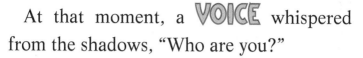 whispered from the shadows, "Who are you?"

I nearly jumped out of my fur! Who said that?

We flipped on the flashlights on our WRIST COMMUNICATORS and looked around. Swiss supernovas—the stands were filled with small aliens! They stared at us with a mixture of curiosity and fear. I suddenly understood—these were the real inhabitants of Lockix, the Eh-Hems!

NOW WE'RE HERE, TOO!

Thea breathed a sigh of relief. "You're the inhabitants of LOCKIX, right? Are you all right? What happened?"

No one answered. In fact, the alien who seemed like the LEADER of the Eh-Hems took a step backward and turned his back to us.

How mousetastically STRANGE!

But then I thought about what we had read in the *Encyclopedia Galactica*, and it all made sense!

I whispered to my friends, "Remember what we learned about the Eh-Hems when we first arrived here? They are a very private species. That's why they're behaving like this—they're **shy**!"

Trap exclaimed, "Good thinking, Gerry Berry! That must be it. You know how to get them to speak to us, right?"

I held up my paws in protest. **"I actually—"**

But Trap pushed me toward the Eh-Hems. "A true captain always knows how to gain the **trust** of a shy and private alien population."

Stinky space cheese, he couldn't be serious!

"Go on, Cousin!" he continued. "We'll all support you from afar."

Then he left me alone in front of the very confused Eh-Hems. **Squeeeak! Why did this sort of thing always happen to me?**

I tried to start a conversation with the aliens. "Hello! Well . . . I . . ."

The leader of the Eh-Hems gave me a look that made me shut my snout.

I glanced toward Thea, who nodded encouragingly. Next to her, Trap was waving his arms like a soccerix fan. Sally gave me a smile and a thumbs-up. Holey space cheese, I couldn't **disappoint** my friends! But what in the universe could I do to gain the trust of these aliens?

I began to think and think and think . . . until I got a fabumouse idea. The best thing is always to tell the TRUTH!

I gathered my C O U R A G E and turned back to the Eh-Hems. "Friends, I am

Umm . . .
wh-what?

79

Geronimo Stiltonix, captain of the spacemice. We landed on Lockix to help you, but instead, we got into a **COSMIC MESS**! We are truly sorry!"

The head of the Eh-Hems stopped glaring at me, cleared his throat, and spoke in a tiny voice. "Eh-hem . . . eh-hem . . ."

I noticed that he was blushing slightly. Those aliens were TREMENDMOUSELY shy!

"Thank you for your honesty, spacemice. We Eh-Hems appreciate those who tell the truth. Now we know that we can trust you."

I squeaked a sigh of relief.

We want to help you!

Thanks, spacemice!

He went on. "My name is Sam Shyguy, and I am the governor of Lockix. Our planet was invaded by the Scaleers just after the Planetary Invisibility System broke. We refused to help fix it, so the deceptiods locked us in here."

Meteoric mozzarella, once the Eh-Hems got over their shyness they were really very COURAGEOUS little aliens!

Thea walked up next to me. "But why didn't you ask for help from neighboring planets?" she asked Sam.

Sam sighed. "We Eh-Hems are very *reserved* aliens, but we are also very **proud**. We have always managed to do everything on our own. We don't know anyone we can trust because our planet has been **INVISIBLE** for so long."

"So that's why there's no spaceport on Lockix," Thea squeaked.

"And there's **INFORMATION** about you missing from the *Encyclopedia Galactica* because you've been isolated for eons," Sally added.

Trap squeaked up. "Yeah, there aren't even any recipe books from Lockix!"

Sam nodded shyly. "Yes, in fact, we Eh-Hems have never really been interested in meeting other aliens. We invented the **PLANETARY INVISIBILITY SYSTEM** because we wanted to prevent anyone from landing on our planet. We have always been **HaPPY** on our own—but now we understand that there are situations we cannot handle alone!"

My friends and I exchanged understanding looks. Then Thea declared, "You aren't alone anymore — now we're here, too!"

Sam's face lit up with a smile, and all the Eh-Hems behind him grinned at us, too.

But now we're here, too!

We isolated ourselves...

My friends and I exclaimed as one, "Spacemice for one, spacemice for all! We will help you!"

Sam was clearly moved. "Thank you, spacemice! Maybe now, with your help, all is not lost . . ."

WE NEED A PLAN!

At that moment, we heard a strange

CREEEAAAK

and suddenly the stadium floor lit up! I nearly jumped out of my fur. Galactic globs of Gouda, what was going on?

I was about to FAINT in fright when Benjamin and Bugsy Wugsy popped out of the megastadium's athlete entrance!

Benjamin cried, "Uncle, we need to tell you something!"

I hugged him tight. "It's MARVEMOUSE to see you, mouselets! But where were you hiding? Are you the ones who lit up the ground just now?"

"After we snuck off, we FOLLOWED

you from afar," Benjamin explained. "When we saw that the Scaleers were bringing you into the megastadium, we looked for a service entrance. We hid down in the room reserved for the space referee."

Benjamin pointed to a **SMALL ROOM** shaped like a lock right above the athletes' entrance.

"Using the *audio system*, we could hear everything!" he went on. "Once we heard that you had befriended the Eh-Hems, we turned on the lights — and here we are!"

Bugsy Wugsy tugged on my tail. "Uncle G, we have some bad news, too. We overheard that the Scaleers are preparing for another **SPACE RAID**!"

I turned as **WHITE** as Martian mozzarella. Green cheesy moons, we couldn't catch a break!

Luckily, Sally squeaked up. "First, we need to get out of here. We can use the SERVICE DOOR that the mouselets came through. It sounds like it's unguarded."

Sam shook his head. "Once we're outside, the Scaleers will simply capture us again!"

Trap scratched his snout thoughtfully. "We need to stick together and defeat the Scaleers using our wits."

"I agree," Thea said. "But HOW?"

AN IRRESISTIBLE CHALLENGE!

I sighed heavily. Rat-munching robots, we didn't have any idea how to OUTSMART the Scaleers!

Just then Sam Shyguy cried, "I've got it! While we were trapped in here, we heard the Scaleer guards chatting . . . and we discovered their weak spot."

"Tell us!" Thea said with a smile. "What is it?"

"We noticed that the Scaleers like to snicker and SNEER a lot," Sam explained. "In fact, there is only one challenge they cannot resist: the Interspace Joke Challenge!"

The **INTERSPACE JOKE CHALLENGE**? Cheesy comets, I had never even heard of it!

My friends were surprised, too. "**WHAT IS THAT?**" they asked together.

From the Encyclopedia Galactica
THE INTERSPACE JOKE CHALLENGE

The most famous team joke competition in the cosmos.

Rules: Each team tells one joke per turn. If the other teams laugh, they pass the round; if not, they are eliminated. (You are not allowed to tickle your opponents!) The final team left after all other teams have been eliminated wins.

Teams are eliminated if:

1. The opposing team does not laugh.

2. They run out of jokes.

3. They don't respect the rules.

Reigning champions: The Scaleers!

Sam explained, "It's the most famous team joke competition in the cosmos! Whoever tells the FUNNIEST jokes wins. A team is eliminated when it runs out of jokes to tell or tells a joke that doesn't make anyone LaUGH. If we challenge the Scaleers, they will surely accept—after all, they're the reigning champions!"

Squeeeak! A joke competition?

Leaping light-years, I never would have thought of that!

Sam added, "I've been thinking about this for a while, but I didn't do anything about it because we Eh-Hems are too shy. But with the spacemice on our side, we can conquer our shyness!"

Trap gave Sam a high five. "I'M IN, FRIENDS!"

"It seems like our best chance to get out of here," Thea added thoughtfully.

"We'll help you, too!" Benjamin exclaimed. "Bugsy Wugsy and I know a ton of fabumouse jokes from school!"

My friends' enthusiasm gave me courage. I shook Sam's hand and said, "Of course

We will challenge them!

Thanks!

we'll help you—let's **CHALLENGE** the Scaleers!"

With that, we called the guards. The INTERSPACE JOKE CHALLENGE was about to begin!

A Daring Deal

The guards led us to the main square of Lockix, where we found ourselves snout-to-trunk with **Claw** again. Solar smoked Gouda, he seemed even more frightening, more wicked, and more *STINKY* than ever!

Next to our space shuttle was an enormouse spacecraft. The Scaleers were preparing for departure — we needed to hurry!

I tried to stand tall as I squeaked, "W-well . . . we spacemice, along with the Eh-Hems, invite you to take part in an Interspace Joke Challenge!"

The leader of the Scaleers snickered. "You will never beat us. We are the reigning galactic champions!"

My whiskers wobbled—I could sense some **cosmic trouble** approaching!

Seeing that my fur was standing on end, Sam gathered his courage and said, "We'll see about that! Here is our condition: If we **win**, you Scaleers need to leave our planet . . . for good."

Claw looked thoughtful for a moment. He turned and whispered something to the other Scaleers, who all nodded their approval back to him. "Interesting . . . All right, but if we win, you will all work for us **FOREVER**!"

Cosmic cheese rays! He couldn't be serious—could he? I wanted to be a writer, not a **space pirate**!

"So, do we have an agreement?" Claw hissed.

I looked at Sam, who was trembling in

his space cape. I knew that we were all **worried**, but what choice did we have? This was the only way to free Lockix!

Sam and I shook Claw's hand and accepted his conditions.

THE DEAL WAS DONE - SQUEAK!

OUT-OF-THIS-WORLD JOKES!

As we got ready to begin the competition, I couldn't keep my knees from **wobbling** like cottage cheese all over again. On the other paw, the Scaleers were tremendmousely calm. They kept elbowing one another and **SNICKERING**.

"Since you're *new* at this, your team can go first," Claw proposed.

Trap began with a classic joke. "What is a cooking robot's preferred condiment? **MOTOR OIL!**"

The Eh-Hems burst out laughing . . . and even the Scaleers couldn't hold back their giggles!

One of the deceptiods was up next. "What's a space pirate's favorite food? LUNAR BARRRRRBECUE!"

Stellar Swiss balls, those Scaleers were really good!

Bugsy Wugsy and Benjamin took a turn. "What did the spacemouse say the first time he tasted Plutonian provolone? That's out of this world!"

All of the aliens snickered. I was so proud of our mouselets!

The competition continued for hours. It turned out that we all knew an enormouse number of jokes!

Haw, haw, haw!

Eventually, Sam Shyguy was up against Fang, a huge Scaleer.

Sam timidly stepped

forward. "What's . . . umm . . . the o-only thing a p-planet could a-ask for?"

Then he stopped. Mousey meteorites! We had to do something, or this would be the end of **LOCKIX**!

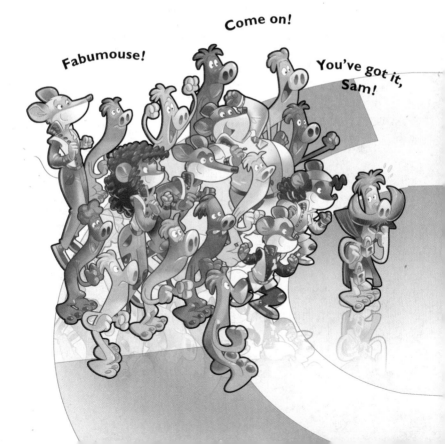

Fabumouse!

Come on!

You've got it, Sam!

We all cheered, "you're fabumouse, Sam! you've got it!"

The supershy alien seemed to collect himself. He looked at us gratefully and repeated, "What is the only thing a PLANET

Ha, ha, ha!

Hee, hee, hee!

Ho, ho, ho!

could ask for? **A LITTLE . . . SPACE!**"

The Scaleers tried to keep their composure, but it was useless—they all burst out laughing.

Swiss-munching spacemice, Sam had done it!

But the competition wasn't over yet. It was **Fang's** turn. The other competitors had already told so many jokes, it was going to be hard to think of another one.

We all stared silently at Fang as he cleared his throat.

Then he **SCRATCHED** his head.

Then he **BLEW** his nose.

In the end, he took a deep breath and began to stutter, "T-two c-cosmobandits e-enter a r-room aaaand . . . aaaaand . . . aaaaand . . ."

We all exclaimed, "**And?**"

And . . . and . . . and . . .

Fang stayed silent. Claw stopped smiling, the Eh-Hems all held their breath. We spacemice looked at one another hopefully.

Fang began to **sweat** and whispered in a tiny voice, "Uh . . . ummm, boss? Um, I've RUN OUT OF JOKES . . . I can't even make anything up. Nothing is coming to mind!"

The Eh-Hems exploded in shouts of joy as Claw glared at Fang.

"We did it!" Trap squeaked.

Bugsy Wugsy and Benjamin high-fived, and Sally cried, "Hooray for the spacemice! Hooray for the Eh-Hems!"

Starry space dust! We had managed to

defeat those fur-raising **space pirates**!

At that moment, Sam held up his hands for silence. "The Scaleers have lost the INTERSPACE JOKE CHALLENGE. As promised, they must leave Planet Lockix at once!"

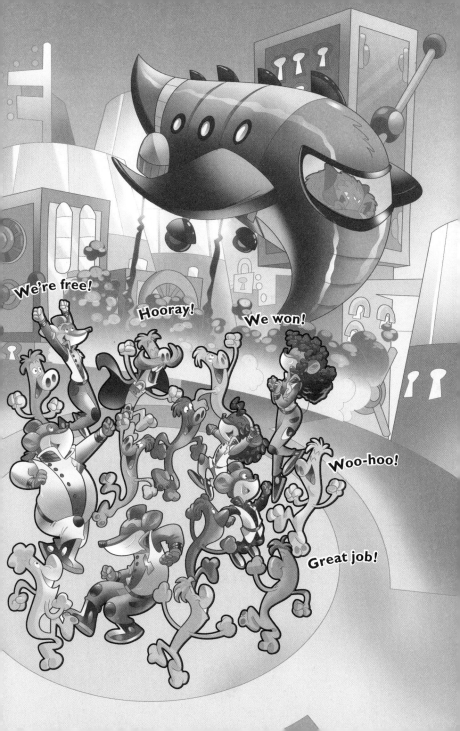

TRUE FRIENDS!

Once the Scaleers finally left the planet, it was time for us spacemice to head home, too.

Sam shook my paw. "We can't thank you enough for your help, spacemice. Without you, we would still be trapped back at the stadium!"

Sally smiled. "Now don't forget, always maintain your Planetary Invisibility System, otherwise you risk having it jam again and—"

But Sam interrupted her. "Oh, there will be no need!"

What in the galaxy was he talking about? "Why not?" I asked.

106

Sam smiled as he explained. "Thanks to you, we now understand that we shouldn't stay so closed off. We need to learn to trust others—that's the only way to meet new aliens who are as nice as you! So we no longer need the PLANETARY INVISIBILITY SYSTEM. We're going to turn it off forever!"

It's been a real pleasure!

Thanks!

"That's *MOUSERIFIC* news!" Thea cried.

Sam continued. "That's not all. We also decided to build a spaceport—that way, you can come back and visit us whenever you want!"

We all hugged one another happily, then said good-bye to our new friends and boarded our EXPLORATION SPACE SHUTTLE.

Leaping lunar cheese balls, it was clear to me that the most important treasure in the whole cosmos is true friendship!

Friendship Is Fortune

We returned to *MouseStar 1*, where Grandfather William and Professor Greenfur greeted us eagerly. They were *curious* to hear the details of our mission.

When I'd finished telling them the story, Grandfather exclaimed, "**Fabumouse job, Grandson!** See? When you try hard, even you manage to do something good!"

Well done, Grandson!

I felt my fur turn red, from the ends of my ears to the tip of my tail. I was **HAPPY** that Grandfather was pleased with me, but

even **HaPPieR** that everything had turned out for the best on Planet Lockix.

Just then Benjamin ran up and gave me an enormouse **hug**. "You're a mouserific captain, Uncle!"

Bugsy Wugsy, Trap, Thea, and Sally all squeezed me in a big group hug and squeaked,

"Hooray For Captain Stiltonix!"

Hooray!

It was wonderful to be surrounded by **SO MANY FRIENDS**!

"All's well that ends well!" I said. "But now I must go change my **SPACESUIT**. I want to get comfortable and—"

Trap interrupted me. "Just a whisker-loving minute! Aren't you forgetting something, Cousin?"

I tried to remember my **URGENT** appointments. Oh, for all the planets out of orbit, nothing was coming to mind!

My friends put their arms around me and led me along. As we walked, I kept **thinking and thinking and thinking** . . .

What had I forgotten?

Cosmic cheese rays, I was concentrating so hard that I didn't even pay attention to where they were taking me!

So, when I lifted my snout up . . .

SQUEEEEEAK! We were back at **Astral Park!**

"Uncle, we can finally **RIDE** the ShatterMousix!" Benjamin exclaimed.

Bugsy Wugsy grinned. "Now that the mission is over, we can go a **million** times!"

"And we'll sit in the front row!" Trap added, nudging me with his elbow.

Oh no— the ShatterMousix!

For the love of space cheese, I had forgotten about the **ShatterMousix**! And now I didn't have any excuse to turn back!

So I got in the line with my friends and waited to board the ride.

After all, even if it was a mousetastically fur-raising experience, being with my friends made me feel more COURAGEOUS. Plus, the adventure on planet Lockix had taught me that being too timid wasn't always a fabumouse idea.

I couldn't wait to put my paws up and have a nice, quiet evening . . . but there's sure to be another stellar adventure on the horizon, or my name isn't Geronimo Stiltonix, captain of the *MouseStar 1*!

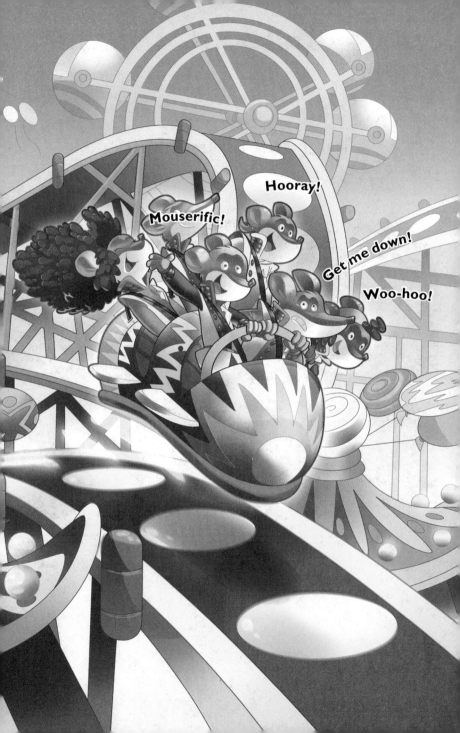

Don't miss any adventures of the Spacemice!

#1 Alien Escape

#2 You're Mine, Captain!

#3 Ice Planet Adventure

#4 The Galactic Goal

#5 Rescue Rebellion

#6 The Underwater Planet

#7 Beware! Space Junk!

#8 Away in a Star Sled

#9 Slurp Monster Showdown

#10 Pirate Spacecat Attack

#11 We'll Bite Your Tail, Geronimo!

#12 The Invisible Planet

Be sure to read all my fabumouse adventures!

#1 Lost Treasure of the Emerald Eye

#2 The Curse of the Cheese Pyramid

#3 Cat and Mouse in a Haunted House

#4 I'm Too Fond of My Fur!

#5 Four Mice Deep in the Jungle

#6 Paws Off, Cheddarface!

#7 Red Pizzas for a Blue Count

#8 Attack of the Bandit Cats

#9 A Fabumouse Vacation for Geronimo

#10 All Because of a Cup of Coffee

#11 It's Halloween, You 'Fraidy Mouse!

#12 Merry Christmas, Geronimo!

#13 The Phantom of the Subway

#14 The Temple of the Ruby of Fire

#15 The Mona Mousa Code

#16 A Cheese-Colored Camper

#17 Watch Your Whiskers, Stilton!

#18 Shipwreck on the Pirate Islands

#19 My Name Is Stilton, Geronimo Stilton

#20 Surf's Up, Geronimo!

#21 The Wild, Wild West

#22 The Secret of Cacklefur Castle

A Christmas Tale

#23 Valentine's Day Disaster

#24 Field Trip to Niagara Falls

#25 The Search for Sunken Treasure

#26 The Mummy with No Name

#27 The Christmas Toy Factory

#28 Wedding Crasher

#29 Down and Out Down Under

#30 The Mouse Island Marathon

#31 The Mysterious Cheese Thief

Christmas Catastrophe

#32 Valley of the Giant Skeletons

#33 Geronimo and the Gold Medal Mystery

#34 Geronimo Stilton, Secret Agent

#35 A Very Merry Christmas

#36 Geronimo's Valentine

#37 The Race Across America

#38 A Fabumouse School Adventure

#39 Singing Sensation

#40 The Karate Mouse

#41 Mighty Mount Kilimanjaro

#42 The Peculiar Pumpkin Thief

#43 I'm Not a Supermouse!

#44 The Giant Diamond Robbery

#45 Save the White Whale!

#46 The Haunted Castle

#47 Run for the Hills, Geronimo!

#48 The Mystery in Venice

#49 The Way of the Samurai

#50 This Hotel Is Haunted!

#51 The Enormouse Pearl Heist

#52 Mouse in Space!

#53 Rumble in the Jungle

#54 Get into Gear, Stilton!

#55 The Golden Statue Plot

#56 Flight of the Red Bandit

#57 The Stinky Cheese Vacation

#58 The Super Chef Contest

#59 Welcome to Moldy Manor

#60 The Treasure of Easter Island

#61 Mouse House Hunter

#62 Mouse Overboard!

#63 The Cheese Experiment

#64 Magical Mission

#65 Bollywood Burglary

#66 Operation: Secret Recipe

#67 The Chocolate Chase

#68 Cyber-Thief Showdown

#69 Hug a Tree, Geronimo

Don't miss any of these exciting Thea Sisters adventures!

Thea Stilton and the Dragon's Code

Thea Stilton and the Mountain of Fire

Thea Stilton and the Ghost of the Shipwreck

Thea Stilton and the Secret City

Thea Stilton and the Mystery in Paris

Thea Stilton and the Cherry Blossom Adventure

Thea Stilton and the Star Castaways

Thea Stilton: Big Trouble in the Big Apple

Thea Stilton and the Ice Treasure

Thea Stilton and the Secret of the Old Castle

Thea Stilton and the Blue Scarab Hunt

Thea Stilton and the Prince's Emerald

Thea Stilton and the Mystery on the Orient Express

Thea Stilton and the Dancing Shadows

Thea Stilton and the Legend of the Fire Flowers

Thea Stilton and the Spanish Dance Mission

Thea Stilton and the Journey to the Lion's Den

Thea Stilton and the Great Tulip Heist

Thea Stilton and the Chocolate Sabotage

Thea Stilton and the Missing Myth

**Thea Stilton and the
Lost Letters**

**Thea Stilton and the
Tropical Treasure**

**Thea Stilton and the
Hollywood Hoax**

**Thea Stilton and the
Madagascar Madness**

**Thea Stilton and the
Frozen Fiasco**

**Thea Stilton and the
Venice Masquerade**

**Thea Stilton and the
Niagara Splash**

**Thea Stilton and the
Riddle of the Ruins**

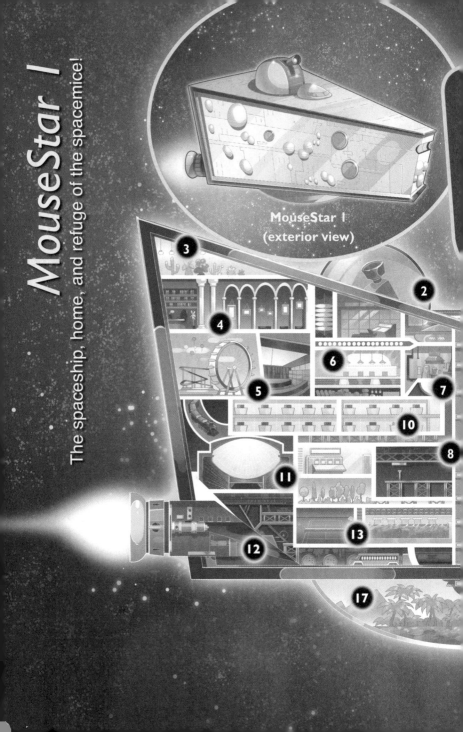

MouseStar 1

The spaceship, home, and refuge of the spacemice!

MouseStar 1
(exterior view)

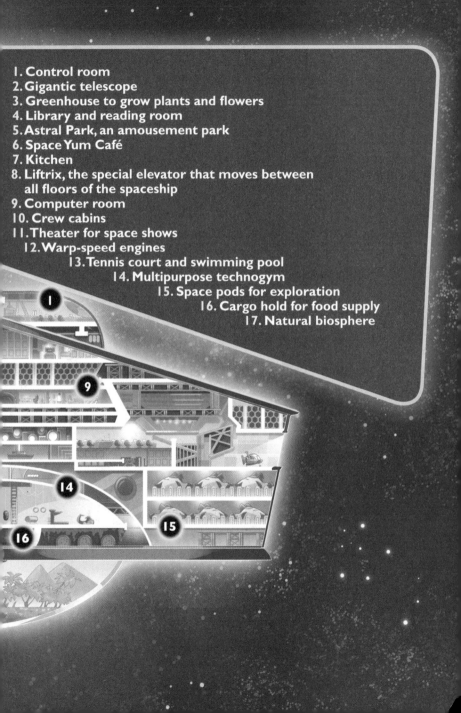

1. Control room
2. Gigantic telescope
3. Greenhouse to grow plants and flowers
4. Library and reading room
5. Astral Park, an amousement park
6. Space Yum Café
7. Kitchen
8. Liftrix, the special elevator that moves between all floors of the spaceship
9. Computer room
10. Crew cabins
11. Theater for space shows
12. Warp-speed engines
13. Tennis court and swimming pool
14. Multipurpose technogym
15. Space pods for exploration
16. Cargo hold for food supply
17. Natural biosphere

*Dear mouse friends,
thanks for reading,
and good-bye until the next book.
See you in outer space!*

In the darkness of the farthest galaxy in time and space is a spaceship inhabited exclusively by mice.

This fabumouse vessel is called the **MouseStar 1**, and I am its captain!

I am Geronimo Stiltonix, a somewhat accident-prone mouse who (to tell you the truth) would rather be writing novels than steering a spaceship.

But for now, my adventurous family and I are busy traveling around the universe on exciting intergalactic missions.

THIS IS THE LATEST ADVENTURE OF THE SPACEMICE!

THE SPACEMICE

GERONIMO STILTONIX

TRAP STILTONIX

THEA STILTONIX

GRANDFATHER WILLIAM STILTONIX

ROBOTIX

BENJAMIN STILTONIX AND BUGSY WUGSY

My dear mouse friends,

Have I ever told you how much I love science fiction? I've always wanted to write incredible adventures set in another dimension, but I've never believed that parallel universes exist . . . until now!

That's because my good friend Professor Paws von Volt, the brilliant, secretive scientist, has just made an incredible discovery. Thanks to some mousetropic calculations, he determined that there are many different dimensions in time and space, where anything could be possible.

The professor's work inspired me to write this science fiction adventure in which my family and I travel through space in search of new worlds. We're a fabumouse crew: the spacemice!

I hope you enjoy this intergalactic adventure!

Geronimo Stilton

PROFESSOR
PAWS VON VOLT